NICKELODEON

Drake & Josh

Go Hollywood

Adapted by Laurie McElroy
Based on "Drake and Josh Go Hollywood"
Teleplay by Dan Schneider

D1636150

SCHOLASTIC INC.
New York   Toronto   London   Auckland   Sydney
Mexico City   New Delhi   Hong Kong   Buenos Aires

ISBN 0-439-89043-8

Published by Scholastic Inc.

SCHOLASTIC and associated logos are trademarks and/or registered
trademarks of Scholastic Inc.

12 11 10 9 8 7 6 5 4 3 2 1   6 7 8 9 10/0

Printed in the U.S.A.
First printing, September 2006

CHAPTER ONE

"Hey! Hey!" Josh Nichols shouted. Where was everyone? He had amazing news to share. "I got in!"

Josh barreled into the kitchen and found his step-sister, Megan Parker, calmly cutting up strawberries and bananas. "Hey, Megan!" Josh waved a letter in the air. Megan wasn't exactly his biggest fan, but this news was too good to keep to himself. "Guess what."

Megan didn't look up. "You finally got chest hair," she said in a bored voice, slicing a strawberry.

"No," Josh said, but he pulled out the neck of his shirt and looked down at his chest just in case. "No." He sighed, then he brightened again. "I got accepted into that creative writing program!"

Megan gazed blankly at him for a second. Creative writing? That's what Josh was babbling about. "Wow," she said, using a voice that let Josh know she was thinking anything else but wow.

Josh's eyes widened in disbelief. "Wow? That's your level of excitement for me?" he asked.

"Sorry." Megan rolled her eyes and flipped her dark brown hair over her shoulder. She gave Josh a fake smile and added in a big, sarcastic squeal, "Wow!!!" She waved her arms in mock excitement. "Now can I get back to my smoothie?"

Josh was determined to make his sister understand just how amazing this was. "C'mon, this writing class is a really big deal," he said. "They only accept five high school juniors every summer, so it's really a prestigious honor to —"

Megan added the banana and strawberry slices to the ingredients already in the blender, then pushed the ON button.

Josh raised his voice and tried to speak over the noise. "Cause I'm starting the class."

Megan stared out the window, counting in her head to be sure her smoothie was blended to perfection. Plus, it had the extra added benefit of torturing Josh — one of Megan's favorite pastimes.

Josh was still talking. "So that when I start, I'll have the —"

Megan hummed to herself. Not hearing. Not caring.

This is fun, she thought, watching Josh get more and more frustrated.

"You can't hear me if you keep making a smoothie," he yelled.

Megan grinned. Her smoothie was finished, but stopping now would be like giving in to her brother, and that wasn't going to happen.

Josh threw his arms up in the air and gave up. He'd find someone else to listen to his amazing news. Megan would have to hear about his writing class another way — like when he turned her into an evil witch in one of his stories.

With a smile, Megan watched him leave. Bugging Josh was just too easy.

Josh's father, Walter, and his stepmother, Audrey, were in the living room. *Finally*, Josh thought, *someone will be excited about my news*. But his parents had other things on their minds.

Walter had a travel brochure spread out in front of him. "Look, we get to stop in Acapulco," Walter said.

"I don't want to go on a cruise," Audrey said with a frown.

"It's too late to cancel," Walter said. "If you didn't want to go, you should have said something three months ago."

"I did," Audrey insisted. She had been telling Walter for months that she didn't want to go on a cruise, but he had booked one anyway.

Josh tried to wait till they finished talking, but he was too excited. "Hey, guess what," he said.

"You finally got chest hair?" Walter asked.

Josh's face fell. "No," he moaned. Why did everyone keep asking him that? "I got accepted into that creative writing class," he said. "I already have my first assignment. My teacher wants me to write a story about my greatest adventure ever." Josh smiled. He was sure he could come up with something creative and exciting — a story that would impress everyone.

But his father was still caught up in the idea of getting Audrey excited about the cruise. "Oh," he said, spotting another selling point on the cruise ship's travel brochure. "And Mazatlán! You're always saying how you want to visit Mazatlán."

"I've never said that," Audrey said.

"Oh, never . . . always . . . what's the difference?" Walter asked.

"Never mind, I'm going to find Drake," Josh said, sitting on the arm of a chair.

"He's taking me on a ten-day cruise and he knows I don't like boats," Audrey said.

"Why don't you like boats?" Josh asked.

"Boats sink," Audrey announced.

"It's not a boat," Walter explained. "It's a ship. And ships don't sink."

Audrey looked at her husband like he was crazy. Did Walter seriously believe that ships couldn't sink? She had just one reply. "*Ti-tan-ic*," she said, stretching out the name of the famous ship.

"That was just a movie," Walter said.

"Based on a *true* story," Audrey answered smugly.

"For real?" Walter asked.

Josh had heard enough. He didn't care about ships, sinking or otherwise. Someone had to be excited about his news. He headed upstairs in search of the guy who was always on his side — his stepbrother, Drake.

*　　　*　　　*

Up in the bedroom he shared with Josh, Drake Parker tuned his electric guitar. Their room stretched from the front of the house to the back, over the garage. It was unfinished, with exposed beams and unpainted wallboard, but Drake liked it that way. He had built a loft bed under the window, bought an old couch and comfy chairs at a yard sale, and filled the walls with posters of his favorite bands, road signs, and old license plates. After Josh's dad married Drake's mom, they had added a bed for Josh.

There was nothing better than kicking back on their couch, feet up on the coffee table, watching the tube or playing video games.

Josh walked in, ready to share his amazing news, but he caught sight of Drake fiddling with the buttons on a high-tech-looking silver and glass box with a silver ball on top. "What is that?" he asked.

"Amplifier for my guitar," Drake answered.

It looked like an amplifier from the future, Josh thought. "It's huge."

"Thanks," Drake said. It was huge — not to mention

hugely cool. "Want to see what it does?" he asked. He couldn't wait to show it off.

Josh's forehead wrinkled. He knew what amplifiers did. He'd heard Drake play his electric guitar a million times. "It just makes your guitar loud, right?"

"Yeah," Drake answered with a sly grin. "But this one does *other things*." He reached over and switched off the room lights. "Are you ready, Josh?"

"Okay," Josh said slowly, wondering what Drake meant by "other things."

Drake flipped a few switches on the amplifier. It lit up and started to hum. It was like it came to life or something. "Okay, watch this," he said.

Drake plucked a string. Not only did Josh hear the note from the amp, but the silver ball on top fired a green laser beam across the room. The beam lasted until the note faded.

"Whoa!" Josh said. His eyes lit up. This was cool!

Drake plucked two strings. This time two laser beams crossed the room in opposite directions.

"How does it do that?" Josh asked.

Drake grinned. "Oh, you've seen nothing, young

man. Watch — a chord." Drake played a chord. Six laser beams — green, pink, yellow, red, blue, and purple — shot across the room in different directions, crisscrossing each other.

"That's insane," Josh yelled. The amp didn't just look like an amp from the future. It *was* one. Josh had never seen anything like it.

Drake launched into a rockin' song. The amp went wild, shooting hundreds of colorful beams around the room. Even Drake was amazed. He was so caught up in the lights and the music that he didn't even hear the phone ring.

"Hello?" Josh answered, straining to hear over the guitar. He tapped Drake with the phone. The light show ended when Drake stopped playing. "It's your band manager," Josh said, handing him the phone.

"Thanks." Drake put his guitar down and grabbed the phone. He had a gig coming up and he couldn't wait to wow the crowd with his new amp.

"Chuck. I just wanted to know what time me and the band should show up," Drake said.

Josh picked up the guitar and plucked one string, then another, watching the laser beams shoot across the room. He stopped when Drake started shouting.

"The gig's canceled?" Drake yelled into the phone. "Dude, that's the third time this month."

Chuck babbled on the other end.

"Yeah, yeah, I've heard it all before, Chuck." Drake shook his head in exasperation. What was the use of having a band manager if he couldn't book them decent gigs? "Look, you want to keep managing my band? Then book us a gig. And it better be someplace good." Drake hung up with a frown. How would he ever make it in the music business with a lame manager like Chuck?

CHAPTER TWO

The next evening, Drake and his band stood on a small stage. Chuck had booked them a gig, but he had totally missed the "someplace good" part of the demand in Drake's last warning.

"Hi. We're really excited to be playing here at the B'nai Shalom Home for the Elderly." Drake grimaced. "I'm Drake Parker."

He and his band looked out over the audience of a dozen senior citizens. The seniors stared back at them with blank expressions. They sat slumped in their chairs. Some of them had oxygen tanks. Others had medicine dripping into their arms. One woman was sound asleep.

Drake had nothing against old people, but when he told Chuck to get them a gig or else, a home for the elderly was definitely not what he had in mind. And Drake's rock-and-roll band was not what the elderly had in mind, either. "We want Wayne Newton!" growled one old man from the front row.

The lady next to him agreed. "Wayne Newton," she shouted, banging her walker on the floor. "Not you."

This is absolutely the worst gig I've ever had, Drake thought. But he was being paid to be here, so he'd give it a try. "This is a song I wrote when I was about fifteen. It's an interesting story because I —"

"Hippie!" yelled the old man, taking in Drake's shaggy brown hair.

"You communist!" shouted the lady, eyeing his vintage logo T-shirt and jeans.

Communist? Drake signaled his band to start playing, but the man wasn't finished heckling. "You ain't no Wayne Newton!"

"Thank you," Drake said. As far as he was concerned, Wayne Newton was colossally lame. His grandparents listened to Wayne Newton. The audience sat and stared while Drake and their band did their best to bring some excitement to their song. It didn't work.

The old man scowled. "Where's my applesauce?" he yelled.

Drake shook his head and kept singing.

"Where's my applesauce?" the man shouted again.

"Would someone please get him his applesauce?" Drake begged.

The woman with the walker turned to the old man and yelled in his ear. "You already ate your applesauce!"

"Then where are my pills?" the man shouted back.

Drake rolled his eyes and kept singing. After a few more seconds, he turned to his bass player and nodded. Maybe the new amp would get the crowd going. Dozens of laser beams fired all over the room. But instead of exciting the crowd, the lights scared them. Drake watched in horror as the audience started screaming and running from the room, holding their hands over their ears.

Drake hadn't realized old people could move so fast. In seconds, they cleared the room. The only one still seated was the woman who was asleep. The music and the screaming hadn't bothered her a bit — she just slept on.

That's it, Drake thought. *Chuck is so fired.*

Josh sat on the couch in his bedroom, his laptop open in front of him and a full plate of grapes at his side. He said the words as he typed: *My Greatest Adventure*.

Josh thought that when he typed the title, the words would start to flow. But they didn't. The cursor blinked. Josh stared. He ate a grape. The cursor blinked some more. He ran his hand through his dark, wavy hair. Was it possible he had never had an adventure?

"I must have done something interesting," Josh said to himself. But he couldn't think of a thing. Not one thing. He sighed and ate another grape, watching the cursor blink, blink, blink.

Fifty grapes later, Josh was still staring at an empty screen.

"C'mon," he said to himself. "My greatest adventure." He must have had at least one adventure in his life. He ate one more grape and then finally got an idea. "Oh, yeah!" he said, snapping his fingers.

Once, when I was nine, Josh typed. *I climbed a tall tree. Imagine my excitement when I happened upon a birds' nest on one of the tall branches.*

Then he realized just how lame his adventure was. "I'm pathetic," he muttered.

Megan suddenly popped up behind him. "Yeah," she agreed.

Josh jumped. How did she always manage to sneak up on him like that? He used his most irritated voice. "Can I help you?" he asked.

"Mom said I could borrow Drake's suitcase," Megan said, heading for the shelf next to Drake's loft bed.

"Why do you need a suitcase?" Josh asked. "Where are you going?"

"Colorado," Megan answered, grabbing the suitcase. "Mom and Dad are letting me take a trip to visit my friend Jessica while they're on their cruise."

"Wait." Josh's eyes widened. "So Drake and I get the house to ourselves for ten days?"

Megan shrugged. Josh was under the impression she cared about what he and her brother had or didn't have. "Guess so."

"Awesome!" Josh said with a big smile. This was going to be great! Just Josh and Drake — no parents, and more important, no Megan.

"Later," Megan said and headed out of the room, but Josh stopped her.

"Wait, Megan," he said. Something was bothering

him. Normally he'd talk to Drake about this, or his dad, but Megan was here. "Can I ask your opinion about something kind of serious?"

Megan rolled her eyes. "Is this about your rash?"

"No!" Josh answered, his shoulders slumping. Maybe Megan wasn't the right person to talk to about this, but he had to talk to *someone*. He kept his eyes on his computer screen. "See, I've been sitting here for two hours and I can't think of one really exciting thing that's ever happened to me. Do you think I'm . . ." his voice trailed off; he hated to say the word. And then he did. "Boring?"

Josh turned toward Megan. She was gone.

"You just walked out?" he yelled.

"I got bored," Megan answered from the hall.

Josh sighed and watched the cursor blink. But he didn't have to stare long. Drake ran up the stairs, holding his guitar, and slammed the bedroom door behind him.

"Hi," Drake said.

"Hey. How'd your gig go?"

"How'd my gig go?" Drake threw his guitar case on his bed and opened his jacket. His T-shirt was covered with applesauce. "The elderly threw food at me."

Josh's forehead wrinkled in confusion. "Why were you playing for old people?" Drake's band was awesome, but they were new and cool and cutting edge. Josh knew there was no way senior citizens would appreciate Drake's music.

"That's my band manager's idea of a good gig," Drake complained. "Boy, I hate my band manager."

Josh thought for a second. Then his face lit up. He looked at Drake.

Drake didn't have to hear the question. He knew what that excited expression on Josh's face meant. "No!" Drake said before Josh could speak.

"Let me be your band manager?" Josh said, asking anyway.

"No."

"C'mon!" Josh jumped to his feet, ready to make his case. "Dude, it would be so great."

Drake held his hands up in front of him and moved around the room, trying to keep Josh at bay. But Josh stayed right on his heels. "No," Drake repeated.

"Dude, it'll be awesome!"

"No." Drake was firm.

"I will do such a great job." Josh followed Drake around the couch.

"No. No. No."

"C'mon, who's going to try harder than your own brother?" Josh pleaded.

"No!" Drake insisted. Josh was a great guy, but he didn't know anything about how to manage a band.

Josh could read Drake's expression, too, and there was no way he was going to give up. "All right, I realize I don't know much about managing a band, but I can learn. And you know that when I put my head to something, I give it a thousand and ten percent."

"No, no, no, no, no." Drake climbed the ladder to his loft bed.

"C'mon." Josh stood at the bottom of the ladder, his hands up under his chin. "Please let me be your band manager. Please," he begged.

Drake knew Josh would keep asking, and asking, and asking, until he drove Drake absolutely crazy. He'd have to let Josh try this. He only hoped it wouldn't be too big a disaster. He threw his arms up in the air. "Okay," he said.

"Okay?" Josh said. Had he heard right?

"Yes." Drake slumped on his bed.

"Yay!" Josh yelled.

"Don't say yay," Drake answered. This wasn't exactly a good thing. If a real band manager couldn't do better than the B'nai Shalom Home for the Elderly, where would Josh be able to book them? Drake wondered if he had just set himself and his brother up for failure.

"No yay," Josh said, but he couldn't stop smiling. This was going to be awesome!

"Why do you want to do this, anyway?" Drake asked. Josh had always been a fan, but he had never talked about managing the band before.

Josh sat in front of his laptop with a sigh. "I'm supposed to write a paper about the greatest adventure of my life. And I haven't really had any great adventures," he explained. "Which got me thinking that . . . well . . . maybe my life's been kind of boring so far. And I don't want to be boring, you know?"

Josh turned to his brother for support. But Drake was sprawled on his bed, sound asleep. The only answer Josh got was a loud snore.

"All right," Josh groaned, shaking his head.

CHAPTER THREE

The next day, Josh sat in the living room trying to think of ways to get Drake's band a contract, while Drake raided the refrigerator. Could it be as simple as calling record companies and asking for a million-dollar record deal? Probably not.

The doorbell rang.

"Hang on a second!" Walter called. He struggled into the room and dropped two heavy suitcases before answering the door.

"Taxi?" asked the driver at the door.

"Right, one second," Walter said, then yelled toward the back of the house. "Honey, taxi's here."

"Okay." Audrey wheeled her own suitcase to the door.

"Hey, Mom. You need some help with those bags?" Drake asked, coming out of the kitchen.

"Please," Audrey said.

Drake nodded at the taxi driver, then pointed toward the bags. "Dude?"

The driver rolled his eyes and reached for the luggage. "So where are you guys headed?" he asked.

"San Diego Marina. We're taking a ten-day cruise," Walter said with a proud smile.

The driver winced. "I hate boats."

Audrey gave Walter an "I told you so" look. Then she turned to Drake. "Megan's plane leaves in two hours. Promise me you'll get her to the airport on time."

Drake nodded casually.

She looked into her son's eyes. "Promise me."

"What, you don't trust me?" Drake asked.

Audrey rolled her eyes. She didn't trust him. Josh could usually be counted on, though. "Josh?"

"No worries," Josh said with a smile.

"Her little friend will be so upset if Megan misses her flight," Audrey said.

"We'll make sure she's on the plane," Josh said.

"Flight seven forty-six to Denver," Audrey said.

Walter tried to hurry her along. "C'mon, honey, we have to go."

Drake and Josh waved good-bye. Now all they had

to do was put Megan on her plane, and they'd have the house to themselves for ten whole days!

Drake grabbed his jacket and car keys. "Well, I'll see you later," he said.

"Where are you going?" Josh asked.

"To get a corn dog," he said, as if the answer should have been totally obvious.

"Okay, but hurry back. We should get Megan to the airport an hour before the plane —"

The door slammed, cutting Josh off. Drake wasn't about to wait around and listen to Josh babble about schedules when there was a corn dog calling his name.

An hour and fifteen minutes later, Josh and Megan paced in front of the door.

Megan checked her watch. "Where is Drake?"

"I don't know," Josh answered.

"I'm going to miss my plane!"

Drake breezed through the front door, eating a corn dog.

"Hey, where have you been?" Josh said.

Drake looked at him with a confused expression. Josh knew where he was. "I told you. I went to the Quigly Mart to get a corn dog."

"It took you over an hour to get *one* corn dog?" Josh said.

What was the big deal, Drake wondered. "I also had a drink."

Megan snatched the corn dog from Drake's hand and threw it on the floor. "Let's go! My plane takes off in forty-five minutes." Drake was lucky she hadn't thrown it at his head.

"Why didn't you just take her in Mom's car?" Drake asked his brother.

"She took her keys. Will you just drive us to the airport, please?" Josh had promised his mom he would get Megan to the airport in time.

"Now!" Megan added.

"All right. Fine." Geez, what was everybody getting so upset about? Drake wondered.

"C'mon. Let's go," Josh said.

Megan grabbed her suitcase and headed for the front door. Drake and Josh ran after her. They climbed into Drake's 1969 Mustang and took off.

Josh had his computer open on his lap.

"Why'd you bring your laptop?" Drake asked.

"I'm watching a DVD of you and your band playing at Medley Park," Josh answered.

"Oh, yeah." Drake leaned over and looked at the screen. "Man, I have good hair," he said with a grin.

Megan fumed in the backseat. Drake had disappeared just when she needed a ride to the airport, and now he was gazing at himself onscreen instead of at the road. "Oncoming truck!" she said.

Drake swerved back into his own lane.

"Wow," Megan said sarcastically. "Hard to believe it took you seven tries to get your driver's license."

Drake narrowed his eyes at her through the rearview mirror. "Six!" he announced.

"Sorry," Megan said, then turned to Josh. "Why are you watching that, anyway?"

"Because I'm managing his band now, so I must familiarize myself with every nuance of Drake's performance skill."

"That shouldn't take too long," Megan said with a frown.

Drake was tired of the snarky comments. He was

doing Megan a favor, after all. And all she did was complain. "You know, I don't have to take that kind of —"

Megan cut him off. "Just focus on your driving. We're barely going to make it." She looked around his car with a disgusted expression. "And do you ever clean this car? It's full of garbage."

First his driving and now his car? What would Megan complain about next? "Everything in this car is very important to me," Drake said.

Megan grasped a dried-up sparrow by its tail feathers. "Like this dead bird?"

Drake checked the rearview mirror. "Awww. Tweeter died," he said.

Megan shuddered and dropped the bird.

Josh noticed a crumpled candy wrapper on the dashboard. "Dude, you really should clean up some of this stuff." He shuffled through the trash around his feet. "Hey, is that my G-O?" He picked up a shiny, silver music player and turned it over. The label read: PROPERTY OF JOSH NICHOLS. "This *is* my G-O." "I haven't been able to listen to my music for three months. You said it got stolen," Josh said with a scowl.

"It did," Drake answered. Wasn't that obvious?

"You didn't say by *you!*"

Drake shrugged. "You didn't ask."

Megan checked her watch again. "Drive faster," she ordered. "My plane leaves in twenty-two minutes."

CHAPTER FOUR

Josh and Megan dashed toward the gate. "Okay, Megan," Josh said, huffing and puffing. "Mom said to give you this credit card."

"Sweet!" Megan said, reaching out to grab it.

Josh pulled it way. "This is only to be used in case of emergencies," he warned her before giving the card back. "Now put it in your backpack."

"Okay. Hold my phone."

Josh took Megan's phone while she slipped the credit card into her backpack. Drake ran up with Megan's boarding pass.

"Here's your ticket," he said.

They listened to a ticket agent make an announcement: "Last call for boarding of flight six forty-seven."

Drake pushed Megan toward the door. They had just made it! "Hurry. Go. Go."

"Okay, have a good trip," Josh said. "Bye!"

Megan hurried to the gate with her suitcase and gave her boarding pass to an agent. She waved good-bye to her brothers just before the ticket agent closed and locked the door.

They watched her go, with huge smiles.

"Well, we got rid of her," Drake said.

Josh grinned. "Yup. Ten days — all to ourselves."

"C'mon," Drake said. "I'm thirsty."

"We should wait here until her plane takes off," Josh said. He didn't know why that was important, but somehow it was. Plus, he liked to watch planes take off and land.

"All right," Drake said. "I'll go get us some sodas. Mocha Cola?"

"Nah, diet." Josh sat down in front of the ticket desk and flipped through a magazine someone had left behind. Then he noticed a TV just over the gate door. A news announcer had just begun a special report:

"We interrupt this program for a special news report. Here in Washington, D.C., I'm standing in front of the U.S. Treasury Building, where a major theft took place earlier this week. According to D.C. Police Chief Daryl Garner, a new United States currency machine was stolen as it was being transferred from

*an armored delivery truck into the Treasury Building.
Eyewitnesses say several men in a dark-colored van
were seen leaving the area —"*

Josh stopped listening when Drake came back with
two giant-size sodas.

"Did her plane take off yet?" Drake asked.

"No." Josh looked out the window. "I think it's just
about to."

Drake looked over Josh's shoulder. "What time does
she get to Denver?"

A passenger, standing at the ticket desk in front of
them, overheard Drake's question. "You mean the plane
that just boarded?" she asked.

"Yeah," Drake answered.

"That flight's going to Los Angeles," she said.

Drake and Josh exchanged uneasy looks. They
couldn't have put Megan on the wrong plane. The
woman was wrong. She had to be.

Drake sat up straighter. "No, it's not."

"It's going to Denver," Josh said confidently, taking
a big sip of his soda. He tried to keep the panic from
his voice. But it didn't work. Seconds later his soda

went flying all over the passenger behind him when Josh threw it in the air and grabbed Drake by the shoulders. "Please tell me that flight's going to Denver," he screamed.

Drake rushed to the ticket desk. Josh ran behind him. They banged into each other and the desk, almost hitting the floor.

"That flight that's about to leave — it's going to Denver, right?" Drake asked. "Say right," he pleaded.

The ticket agent shook her head. "No, this is flight six forty-seven to Los Angeles." She pointed to the electronic sign behind her.

Drake and Josh eyed each other with horror. The agent checked her computer. "The Denver flight number is seven forty-six."

"Oh." Drake suddenly realized what they had done. "Yeah," he said, almost in a whisper.

Josh turned to him, totally freaked out. "Oh, yeah?" he yelled. "You put our eleven-year-old little sister on a plane to the wrong city!"

Drake was freaked out enough. He had to calm Josh down so they could figure out what to do. "All right, this is not a time to panic."

"It's a perfect time to panic!" Josh yelled.

They turned back to the ticket agent. She would help them. She had to.

"You've got to stop that plane," Josh said.

"That's impossible," she answered.

"Why? Just call the pilot and tell him to turn the plane off and not to fly away," Drake said.

Josh pointed to Drake and bobbed his head up and down like a bobble-head doll, pretending to turn a key and shut off the plane. What could be easier?

"I'm sorry," the agent said. "But once the doors to the plane have been closed, the flight cannot be stopped from taking off."

Drake and Josh stared at each other for a second, then turned back to the agent. She was starting to look at them as if they were crazy. It was time to step back and try a new tactic.

"Okay," Josh said.

Drake nodded. "We understand."

"We will respect your rules," Josh said carefully, but he couldn't hide the terror in his voice. They had just made a huge mistake. They were going to be in trouble — *big* trouble. Bigger than they had ever been in before. And what about Megan? Would she know what to do when she landed in Los Angeles? She was the scariest person Josh had ever met, but that was in the comfort of her own home. She was just a little girl after all.

"Let's go home, Josh," Drake said.

"Certainly," Josh agreed, stepping away from the desk.

But they both knew they weren't going home. The brothers didn't even have to talk about it. They walked a few steps away from the desk to make the ticket agent believe they were really leaving. Then they ran full speed toward the door.

"Security! Security to gate 9A," the agent yelled into a microphone.

Drake and Josh pounded on the locked door, trying to get it to open. Trying to get someone — anyone — to hear them and stop the plane.

"Stop the plane," Drake yelled. "You've got to stop the plane. Please."

"Stop the plane," Josh added. "Let us through! We've got a tween sister on the loose!"

Airline workers and passengers rushed toward the

gate and tried to pull the brothers away from the door. The ticket agent continued to call for security.

"Megan!" Drake yelled. Someone was dragging him by the shoulders. He pushed him off and pounded on the door again. "Stop the plane!"

Airport police rushed to the scene and dragged the brothers away.

"Stop the plane!" Drake yelled. "Ow! My legs."

Josh was being carried away by three men. He tried to kick loose, but they had him in a tight grip. "Do you have a permit for this?" he screamed. He couldn't see Drake. He didn't know what was happening, but whatever it was, it wasn't getting Megan off that plane.

Megan kicked back in her seat and sipped a soda. She stopped flipping through her magazine when the captain made an announcement:

> "We've just reached our cruising altitude of fifteen thousand feet, so sit back, enjoy your flight, and we should arrive in Los Angeles a few minutes ahead of schedule."

Los Angeles? That couldn't be right. Megan was going to Denver. She tapped a flight attendant on the shoulder.

"Yes?"

"I think the pilot just made a mistake," Megan smiled. "This plane's going to Denver, right?"

"No, we're en route to Los Angeles."

Megan stopped smiling and swallowed. "Los Angeles?"

"Mmm-hmm."

"Not Denver?"

"No."

The flight attendant went back to pouring drinks while Megan seethed. Her brothers had put her on the wrong plane. "Those idiots," she said to herself.

Airport police escorted Drake and Josh back to the gate.

"All right, boys," said the officer in charge. "I hope you learned a little something today about how seriously we take airport security."

Drake rubbed his arm. "Oh, we learned."

"Your security is shockingly thorough," Josh muttered.

"We do our best," said the officer. "Have a nice day." Then he turned to Josh. "And good luck with that rash."

Josh rolled his eyes. "Yeah, thanks." He watched the officers walk away, still in a panic about Megan. "Okay, now what do we do?" he asked Drake. "How do we find Megan?"

"Relax," Drake said. He took out his cell phone and started dialing. "I'll call her cell phone and tell her that when she lands in L.A., she should get on another flight back to San Diego."

"Yeah," Josh smiled, suddenly relieved. Why hadn't they thought of that before?

They both heard Megan's cell phone ring — in Josh's pocket.

Josh's face fell. This was getting worse and worse. He reached into his pocket and answered Megan's phone. "Hello?" he said, feeling kind of queasy.

"You forgot to give her cell phone back?" Drake yelled into his cell. "That's great. That's awesome," he sneered.

Josh yelled back. This was all Drake's fault. First he almost made them miss the flight, then he rushed

Megan through the gate — the wrong gate. "Don't you give me your attitude," he said into the phone. "I didn't fly her off to the wrong city." He snapped the phone closed and turned his back on Drake.

"Don't you hang up on me," Drake said, still talking into the phone.

Josh shook his head and grabbed Drake by the arm. "Just come on," he said, walking toward the ticket agent.

The agent grabbed a can of pepper spray and pointed in the direction of the guys. She wasn't taking any chances. What if they went crazy again? "Yes?" she said.

"We need two tickets on the next fight to Los Angeles," Josh said.

"We're going to L.A.?" Drake asked.

Josh slapped his emergency credit card down on the desk. "We're going to L.A." Josh answered.

They'd find Megan.

They had to.

CHAPTER FIVE

Drake and Josh dodged a passenger stowing a carry-on bag in the overhead compartment and looked for their seats.

"Okay, let's see." Drake checked his ticket stub. "26E. Here it is." He sat in the middle seat of an empty row. "Where are you?"

"27B," Josh answered, moving one row back. "Right here." He sat in the middle seat of an empty row, too. "Dude, this is great," he said. "I love having a whole row to myself."

"Excuse us," he heard someone yell in a loud Southern accent. "Excuse us." Josh looked up to see a large man and even larger woman shoving their way down the aisle, carrying too many bags and a bucket of fried chicken.

"Where's our seats at, Herb?" yelled the woman. Her voice was as large as her body.

"I'm trying to figure that out," Herb yelled back.

Josh watched them walk toward him and closed

his eyes. "Anything but 27, anything but 27," he chanted.

Herb read his ticket stub. "Let's see . . . 27," he announced.

"Yeah, thanks," Josh muttered under his breath. The minute he thought things couldn't get any worse, they did.

Herb stood over Josh. "A and C. C'mon, Darla," he said.

Josh tried to get out of Darla's way, but she pushed past her husband and climbed right over Josh, landing half on his lap and banging him in the head with her bag. Josh leaned over into Herb's seat to get out of Darla's way. But Herb chose that moment to sit down, landing on Josh's head. Josh wiggled out from under Herb, but he was totally squished. He watched two beautiful girls walk down the aisle and sit on either side of Drake. Josh didn't have to see his brother to know that he had a huge smile on his face.

Josh couldn't think about Drake's good luck for long. Soon there was more shouting in his ear.

"Herb," Darla yelled.

"What?"

Did these people ever speak in a normal tone of voice? Josh wondered.

"Hand me my ointment."

Herb reached into his pocket, poking Josh in the face with his bucket of chicken. But Darla couldn't wait. She leaned over Josh, crushing him, and grabbed it out of Herb's pocket herself.

"Uh-oh," Josh said to himself, as soon as he could breathe again. *Ointment.* Whatever problem he was sitting next to. It couldn't be good.

Megan looked out the window as her plane landed in L.A. She wheeled her suitcase behind her as people rushed off the plane. But Megan was in the wrong city. *What do I do now?* she wondered. Then she spotted a ticket agent behind a desk in the terminal.

"Hi," Megan said with a smile.

"Can I help you?"

"Well, see, I wasn't supposed to fly here to Los Angeles, but my two boobish brothers put me on the wrong plane, so can you please put me on a flight to Denver?" she asked sweetly.

"Let me check the computer and see what's available," the agent answered.

"Cool!" *This is going to be easy,* Megan thought. *And I bet those boobs are all panicked — if they're even smart enough to know they put me on the wrong plane.*

"Uh-oh," said the agent.

That didn't sound good. "What?" Megan asked.

"Denver's experiencing severe thunder storms, so all flights there have been canceled until the weather's cleared."

Megan sighed. "Okay," she said. "I guess I'm spending the night in L.A."

"Can I help you arrange a ride somewhere?"

"Yeah," Megan smiled. "That would be awesome."

The agent picked up the phone. "Taxi or limo?" she asked.

Megan thought for a minute, then grinned. Spending the night in L.A. might not be so bad. "Limo," she answered.

Josh was squeezed in between Herb and Darla. They banged Josh in the face every time they passed their bucket of chicken back and forth. Darla caught sight of something on her arm and stopped gnawing on her chicken wing.

"I'll tell you what," she yelled to Herb. "When we land, you had better take me to a doctor to check out this sore."

"That sore ain't nothing," Herb yelled back. "Forget it."

"It is, too, something." Darla turned to Josh. "Hey, boy, don't you think this sore ought to be seen by a doctor?"

Josh was forced to look at the oozing, ointment-covered mess on Darla's arm. "I really wouldn't know," he mumbled, trying not to gag.

But Darla grabbed a drumstick and moved on to another topic. "Did you get the dipping sauce?" she asked.

Herb slurped the skin off of a chicken wing. "No. They only give you the dipping sauce with the chicken strips."

"Oh, yeah," Darla whined. "The world would just come to an end if I dunked this chicken leg into some dipping sauce."

"Why don't you shut up," Herb yelled back.

Josh wondered if his eardrums would survive an entire flight sitting between these two screamers, then he spotted an empty seat a few rows ahead. "Hey," he said to the flight attendant. "Can I please move to that row up there?"

"Sure, go ahead," she answered.

Josh grabbed his laptop case and tried to climb over Herb, but Herb was intent on protecting his chicken. Josh tripped over Herb's big feet and landed with a bang in the middle of the aisle. He passed Drake on the way to his new seat. Of course, Drake was having a great conversation with two beautiful girls while Josh had been stuck between the chicken-slurping, ointment-oozing, loud-yelling Herb and Darla.

"How ya doing?" Josh asked.

Drake looked away from beautiful girl number one. "Great!" he said. "You?"

"Bad," Josh answered. For one brief second, he thought Drake might offer to trade seats, but brotherly love only goes so far.

"See you later," Drake said, and turned to beautiful girl number two.

Josh moved up to his new row. There was no beautiful girl waiting for him, but there was an empty seat.

Two even. Just one guy sat in the window seat. He looked serious and maybe even a little mean, but he couldn't be anywhere as cranky as Herb and Darla.

"What's up?" Josh asked, dropping into his seat. "I'm Josh."

The guy's expression made it clear that he didn't want to talk. "Deegan," he snapped. "How are you?"

Josh noticed Deegan's earphones. He was fiddling with a small silver music player. "You have a G-O." Josh held up his own with a smile. "That's cool. Me, too."

Deegan glared at Josh, then pulled his ear buds out with an angry sigh. "That's great."

"How many songs does yours hold?" Josh asked.

Deegan's eyes narrowed. Wasn't this kid ever going to shut up? "I don't know."

Josh finally got the message. He put his G-O down on the empty seat between them and looked for someone else to talk to — someone nice.

The captain made an announcement:

"This is the captain. Just letting you know that we'll be starting our descent into Los Angeles in just a few moments."

Josh heard Darla's voice from a few rows behind him. Actually, the whole plane heard Darla's voice.

"I have to go to the toilet," she yelled.

"Well, who's stopping you?" Herb answered.

Darla walked toward the front of the plane just as the pilot made another announcement.

"Looks like we're about to hit some tur-bulence. Please fasten your seat belts."

The plane shook. Darla wobbled between the rows and tried to stay on her feet, hitting a couple of passengers in the head. "Dang it!" she yelled. The plane shook even harder, then shuddered. Darla fell right on top of Josh. She flailed her arms and legs in the air, trying to stand again, while Josh tried to get out from under her.

"Help me!" Josh yelled. "Help me!"

Minutes before her brothers' plane landed, Megan stood in the gate area waiting for her limo driver. She spotted a man carrying a sign with her name on it.

"Hi," she said.

"Hello," said the driver. "Are you Miss Megan?"

"That's me," Megan said.

"I am Ah'lee," he said with a smile. "Your limousine awaits you."

"Awesome," Megan said with a smile.

"And where may I drive you today?" Ah'lee asked.

"I'm not sure." Megan didn't know anything about hotels in Los Angeles, but she knew she deserved the best. "What's the best hotel in Los Angeles?" she asked.

"Ah, that would be the Chambrulay. It is a beautiful hotel, right by the beach."

Megan passed her luggage to Ah'lee. "Let's go," she said.

CHAPTER SIX

Drake and Josh walked out of the jetway, their eyes peeled for Megan.

"You see Megan anywhere?" Josh asked anxiously.

"No. You think she left the airport?" Drake looked around. Where would an eleven-year-old go, all alone in L.A.? Then he remembered they were talking about Megan. "She could be anywhere by now."

"Don't freak out," Josh said. "She's got my cell phone number. Let's just hang here until she calls." Josh pulled Megan's cell phone out of his pocket, and the brothers sat, staring at the phone. It didn't ring.

The minutes ticked by. Still no call.

"I hope she's okay," Josh said with a concerned sigh.

"Man," Drake said. He was really starting to worry. "Where could she be?"

At that moment, Megan was pulling up to the coolest hotel in Los Angeles in her white stretch limousine.

Ah'lee held the door open for her while bellhops rushed forward to take her luggage and bring her lemonade. Megan grinned.

"So, you like the Chambrulay?" Ah'lee asked.

Megan looked around. This place was awesome. "I *like* the Chambrulay," she said.

A bellman led Megan to her room. "Welcome to the Presidential Suite," he announced, opening the doors. "I think you'll find the room to your liking."

Megan walked into the fanciest hotel suite ever. It was huge — almost as big as her whole house in San Diego. There were two giant plasma-screen TVs, a state-of-the-art stereo system, flowers all over the place, and an amazing view of L.A. and the Pacific Ocean. She even had her own private terrace. Megan had asked the desk clerk for the best room in the hotel, and the best was what she got.

It was awesome, but Megan tried to play it cool. "This will work," she said.

As soon as the bellman left, Megan explored the room. She started by jumping on her king-size bed like it was a trampoline, singing along with the music that blasted from the stereo. Then something else caught her eye. She muted the stereo and walked over to a small refrigerator and opened it up. It was full of waters and sodas, candy bars, nuts, and all kinds of snacks Mom said were too expensive.

"A fridge filled with awesome snacks!" she said out loud. "Why doesn't everyone stay here all the time?"

She grabbed a bag of nuts and her bathing suit, and prepared for an afternoon of working on her tan.

Drake and Josh were still at the airport, still staring at the cell phone, getting more and more worried with each minute that passed.

"Why hasn't she called?" Josh asked, frowning.

"I don't know," Drake said anxiously.

Finally, the phone rang.

"It's ringing!" Drake said.

Josh rolled his eyes. "I hear the ringing." He pressed a button. "Hello, Megan?" he said into the phone. "Where are you?"

"At a hotel." Megan was hanging out on one of her private terrace's comfy lounge chairs. Room service had just delivered a smoothie.

"What are you doing at a hotel?" Josh asked.

"Kicking back. Having a smoothie," Megan answered. "What have you guys been doing?"

"What have we been doing?" Josh yelled into the phone. How could Megan be so calm? "Well, first, we put you on the wrong plane!"

"Yeah," Megan answered. "Congrats on reaching a new level of idiocy."

Drake couldn't wait anymore. He only heard Josh's side of the conversation, and that wasn't enough. "Where is she?" he asked Josh.

"What hotel are you at?" Josh asked Megan.

"The Chambrulay — Presidential Suite. And it is definitely *sweet*," she answered.

"Okay, Megan, you stay put. We'll be there as soon as we can," Josh said.

"You guys are here in L.A.?" Megan asked. How did her dorky brothers manage to get themselves to L.A.? she wondered.

"Yes! Now, don't move," Josh said.

Megan looked around her and gave a slight snort. As if she would leave! "Don't worry," she said.

"Let's go get a cab," Josh said. "She's at the Chambrulay Hotel."

"Wait, where is the Chambrulay?" Drake asked.

"I don't know." Josh spotted his seatmate by the baggage claim and rushed over to him. "Hi," he said.

Deegan looked at Josh, then looked away. Why was this kid still bothering him?

"Would you happen to know where the Chambrulay Hotel is?" Josh asked.

Deegan wasn't any nicer off the plane than on it. "Santa Monica. By the beach," he snapped.

"Thanks," Josh said.

Drake grabbed Josh's arm and ran toward a down escalator. "Let's go."

They didn't notice the huge guy wearing a black beret going up on the other side. The guy zeroed in on Deegan and led him to a bathroom where they could talk privately.

"How was your flight?" the man asked.

"All right, Brice," Deegan answered.

Brice looked over his shoulder, then checked the bathroom to make sure no one could hear or see them. "Let's see it," he said.

Deegan pulled his G-O out of his pocket and handed it over.

"Good," Brice said with a smile. "Now, we just better hope that —" Brice stopped in the middle of his sentence when he turned the G-O over. "Who's Josh Nichols?" he asked, reading the label.

Deegan's face fell. "What do you mean?"

Brice showed Deegan the back of the G-O.

Deegan snatched it out of Brice's hands and moaned. "This isn't it!" he yelled.

"You said you had it." Brice moved forward. He loomed over Deegan, his hands balled into fists.

"I did!" Deegan insisted. "This must have gotten switched on the plane. A lady fell on this kid and . . ." Deegan realized who had his G-O. "The kid," he said.

"What kid?"

Deegan pointed to the PROPERTY OF JOSH NICHOLS label. "This kid. He sat in my row. I got his G-O, and he's got ours."

"This is great," Brice said. "He could be anywhere."

"Calm down — I know exactly where he is," Deegan said with a satisfied smile. He and Brice would have to pay Josh Nichols a visit.

CHAPTER SEVEN

Drake and Josh asked their driver to step on it, and he did. They screeched to a stop in front of the Chambrulay Hotel.

Drake jumped out of the car and threw some cash at the driver. "C'mon," he said to Josh, "let's go find Megan's room."

"Okay, but . . ." Josh hesitated.

"What?" Drake asked. They had flown to L.A., spent hours in the airport waiting for Megan to call, and now Josh was saying, "Okay, but . . ."?

"I have to pee so bad," Josh said with a grimace.

Drake stifled a groan. "Can't you hold it?"

"Yeah," Josh said, but his body told him that that was the wrong answer. "No, I can't."

Drake threw his arms up in the air. "Fine, go pee. When I find Megan's room, I'll call your cell and give you the room number."

"Right." Josh took off in a fast run.

He was washing his hands in the men's room when a cool-looking L.A.-kind-of-guy walked in, talking on a cell phone headset.

"No, no, no!" he said. "This is unacceptable, David." He listened for a second, then talked some more. "I have every right to be ticked off! TRL goes live from Hollywood, tomorrow."

TRL — as in TRL on MTV? Josh listened as the guy walked into a stall, still talking.

"Dude, I need a music act."

Music act. Josh's eyes lit up. He fumbled with a towel and dried his hands. He had the perfect music act for TRL, but he had to hurry before the guy left.

"Yeah, and it better be somebody good," the guy was saying. "Oh, come on, David. Excuses aren't going to help."

Josh pulled his bag over his head, hitting himself in the forehead, and whipped out his laptop. He was all thumbs, trying to turn on his computer.

"No, you did the same thing last year with Gwen Stefani," the MTV guy said. "Dude, you can't just cancel a music act a day before a show. You do this and you are going to ruin your reputation at MTV. You want that to happen? Then give me a music act."

This is exactly the kind of break that Drake needs to get a record deal, Josh thought.

"Oh, sure," the MTV guy said. "How am I going to book Usher for tomorrow? He's in Japan. Try again."

Josh clicked on the DVD drive, and the video of Drake's band performing in Medley Park started to play. He turned the volume up as high as it would go. Drake really rocked the park that day. He'd be awesome on TRL!

The MTV guy was still talking. "David, no," he said. "You are making me physically ill."

Josh had exactly what this guy needed to feel better. Just wait till that guy saw Drake in action.

"I'll call you back," the guy said, ending his call.

Josh pretended to be nonchalantly hanging in the bathroom.

The guy picked up the laptop. He stared at Josh.

"Oh," Josh said all innocently. "That's my laptop."

"Yeah, weird," the guy said with a knowing

expression. He had been approached by band managers in a thousand different ways, but this was the first time anyone had ever tried to get him to sign a band in a men's room. If he weren't desperate for an act, he wouldn't even listen. But he *was* desperate.

Josh held the laptop open while the MTV producer — Mitch — watched Drake finish his song on screen.

"Okay," Josh said. "Tell me Drake's not awesome."

"He's good," Mitch agreed.

"He's *great*," Josh said.

"He's very good, but —"

Josh had to stop him before he got to the "but." Josh would do anything for Drake, and this was something Drake wanted more than anything in the world. "Look, I know Drake's not a big star, but he's going to be," Josh said, speaking from his heart. "You saw him perform. C'mon. You need to book a music act, and Drake needs a shot. Just give him three minutes on TRL. And when he wins his first Grammy, I swear he'll thank you for giving him his first real break."

"I would never in a million years book an unsigned artist on TRL," Mitch said.

Now Josh wanted to hear him say "but." "But . . ." Josh said, leading him on.

Mitch threw his hands up in the air. "But I'm going to."

"Woo-hoo-hoo!" Josh squealed.

"You have Drake at Sunset Studios tomorrow at four o'clock for sound check," Mitch said.

Josh nodded. "Sunset Studios. Four o'clock. Sound check," he repeated. Inside he howled silently. Drake was going to be on MTV!

"He goes on at five-thirty," Mitch said as he left the bathroom.

This was the most exciting thing that had ever happened to Josh. And the best thing about it? He was doing something amazing for his brother. Josh couldn't hold it in anymore. He had to scream.

Minutes later, after Josh found his way to the Presidential Suite, Drake was screaming, too.

"Can you believe it?" Josh asked, with a huge smile on his face.

Drake was still screaming.

"TRL, baby!" Josh yelled.

Drake opened his arms wide. "Hug me, brother!"

He leaped into Josh's arms. Both guys screamed some more while Josh swung Drake around.

Megan watched it all with an amused expression. The idea of Drake and his band on TRL was pretty cool, but Megan wasn't about to let her brothers know she was impressed. "Okay, you guys have your little love fest," she said, flipping her hair over her shoulder and heading for the door. "I'm going down by the pool to work on my tan. Throw me my phone."

Josh tossed her the cell phone with a warning. "Do not leave this hotel."

Megan shrugged. Secretly she was glad her brothers had flown to L.A. to make sure she was okay, but she wasn't about to let them know that, either.

Drake's mind raced with everything he had to do before appearing on TRL tomorrow. "I have to call my band and tell them to drive up here tomorrow."

"Already did it," Josh said. "Am I a good band manager or what?"

"The best," Drake said, nodding. "Man, I cannot believe you booked me on TRL."

"What song are you going to do?" Josh asked.

"I'm not sure," Drake answered.

"Then let's listen to all of them and pick the best one," Josh said, pulling out his G-O.

"You have all my songs on your G-O?" Drake asked. He couldn't believe it. Not only was Josh his biggest fan, but he was turning out to be a great manager.

"Of course," Josh answered. "Oh — I've got a couple on my laptop," he remembered. "Give me a second to download them."

Josh connected his G-O to his laptop while Drake wandered over to the refrigerator Megan had discovered earlier. He grabbed a can of soda, then noticed the price list on the top of the fridge.

"Whoa. Six bucks for one can of soda?" he said. He thought about putting it back, then reconsidered. "I'm worth it," he decided.

Josh was still trying to get his laptop and G-O to talk to each other. "This is weird."

"What?" Drake asked, looking over his shoulder.

"Something's wrong with my G-O. Where's my playlist?" He hit some keys on the G-O. "I can't find any of my music."

"Try accessing them from your laptop," Drake suggested.

The brothers leaned in to look at the laptop's screen. Suddenly it was filled with numbered codes and pictures of money. Words like *U.S. Federal Reserve and Treasury* scrolled across the screen, followed by *classified*.

"United States Department of Treasury?" Josh murmured.

"What is that — a band?" Drake asked.

Josh stared at his brother in confusion. "I don't think so," he said thoughtfully. He had heard something on the news about the Treasury Department, but he couldn't quite remember what it was.

The hotel room door slowly opened behind them. Drake and Josh were so focused on the laptop that they didn't notice Deegan and Brice slip into the room.

They scowled when they saw that the G-O was connected to the laptop. They had to get that G-O back before Drake and Josh figured out what was on it. Otherwise, they'd have to find a way to make these guys disappear — permanently.

CHAPTER EIGHT

Josh read the words scrolling across his computer screen. "Classified U.S. Treasury codes," he said. "Hey, look," he said. "It's a picture of a hundred dollar bill.

Deegan and Brice exchanged disturbed looks. This wasn't good. Not only did they have to get the G-O back, but Josh was about to figure out what they were up to.

Josh still didn't know that Deegan and Brice were behind him — waiting and watching. Neither did his brother.

"Okay, so why do you have diagrams of money on your G-O?" Drake asked.

"I'm thinking this isn't my G-O," Josh said.

Brice stepped forward. "I'm thinking your right," he growled.

Drake and Josh whipped around to find Deegan and Brice staring at them from across the room. And they didn't look friendly.

"Who are you?" Drake asked.

Josh recognized Deegan. "Hey, weren't you on our plane?"

Deegan nodded.

Brice stepped forward, a threatening look on his face. "Give us the G-O," he ordered.

"Why?" Josh asked.

"Because he said to," Deegan answered. What was with this kid and the questions?

Deegan and Brice moved toward the brothers. Drake and Josh both took a step back.

"Give him the G-O," Drake said. He didn't know what was going on, but these guys meant business.

"No," Josh said. "I think these guys are up to no good."

"Is that what you think?" Brice asked.

While Josh was focused on Brice, Deegan reached forward and snatched the G-O out of his hand.

"Hey, give that back." Josh made a move toward Deegan, but Brice shoved him out of the way. Josh finally realized that these were seriously bad guys.

Drake just wanted to get himself and his brother away from them. He tried to pretend that there was nothing unusual about two guys — one of them huge and both of them extremely threatening — breaking into their room and demanding Josh's G-O. But his voice shook. "Okay, well, we have to go . . ." His voice trailed off. He couldn't think of an excuse to get out of there.

Josh jumped in with the first thing that popped into his mind. ". . . get haircuts," he added.

"Haircuts. Yes," Drake agreed. He reached over and messed up Josh's hair. "Look at this hair," he said.

Josh ran his hands through his hair, so that it stood up over his head. "Unruly is what it is," he said, nodding.

"What's wrong with your hair?" Deegan asked.

Brice glared at his partner. "There's nothing wrong with his hair," he said.

"That's what I'm saying," Deegan agreed.

Drake started to edge past them. "Yeah. Well, uh, we're just going to RUN!" he shouted, hoping Josh would run along with him.

They tried to plow their way through Brice and Deegan, but Brice grabbed them both around the neck. Drake ducked under his arm, only to find Deegan in front of him, ready to fight. Josh was forced backward by Brice, who picked him up and swung him in the air like he was a rag doll.

"Drake, I've been lifted," Josh yelled. He tickled Brice under his arms, and the big guy was forced to drop him.

There was a knock on the door and a maid walked in. "Housekeeping."

She startled everyone. For a second, Deegan and Brice froze. Drake jumped on a chair and it tipped over, getting closer to the door. Josh was able to spin Brice around and knock him into another chair.

Josh kicked into the air and tried to give a ferocious, karate scream. It came out more like a high-pitched giggle, but it was enough to make Deegan and Brice do a double take. Josh followed Drake out the door, but on the way he grabbed the G-O out of Deegan's hand.

Deegan and Brice found themselves face-to-face with the maid. "You didn't see anything," Brice snarled.

Deegan pulled a hundred dollar bill out of his pocket and held it in front of her.

"I didn't see anything." The maid took the money, then watched them run out the door after Drake and Josh.

Drake and Josh ran down twenty flights of stairs and burst out of the hotel's front doors.

"Josh, c'mon," Drake yelled.

Josh came to a sudden stop, holding his side. "I can't," he huffed. "I can't run anymore."

"Dude, those guys are right behind us! This is no time for wheezing."

Josh rolled his eyes in frustration. It wasn't as if he had a choice. "Like I enjoy wheezing," he said. But he stopped when he saw Deegan and Brice get off the elevator and head in his direction. "Here they come," he groaned.

Drake looked around. There was no way they could outrun those guys. He spotted a car, a red Viper, waiting to be parked by the hotel's valet. "C'mon!" He ran to the car, slid over the trunk, and did a one-handed vault into the driver's seat.

"What are you doing?" Josh yelled.

"Get in!"

Deegan and Brice ran out of the hotel. Panicked, Josh looked over his shoulder and vaulted into the passenger seat, like vaulting into cool sports cars was something he did every day. "How'd I do that?" he asked.

"Just hang on." Drake turned the key and the engine roared to life.

"Get back here," Brice yelled. He and Deegan were almost at the Viper.

Drake put the car into gear and hit the gas. He tore out of the hotel driveway, tires smoking.

CHAPTER NINE

Drake flew down the street.

Josh grabbed on to the dashboard. They were going way too fast, and Drake wasn't the world's greatest driver. "Dude, slow down!" he said.

"You want those goons to catch us?" Drake answered, checking the rearview mirror.

Josh turned around. Deegan and Brice were behind them in a dark-colored sedan. They were gaining on the Viper. "Speed up!" Josh yelled, suddenly changing his mind.

Drake downshifted and hit the gas. The car hit 60, then 70 miles an hour. There was a little more distance between them and the bad guys. "Man, why'd they want your G-O so bad?" Drake asked.

Josh was starting to figure it out himself. "They don't want mine," Josh explained. "They want theirs. Mine must have gotten switched with that guy's on the plane."

"So why are they chasing us?" Drake asked,

confused. "I thought they got theirs back from you already."

"Yeah, but I got it back from them," Josh said with a satisfied smile, holding up Deegan's G-O.

Drake did a double take. Was Josh crazy? "Why'd you do that?"

"Because I think those guys are up to something illegal."

Drake couldn't believe it. Those two goons were chasing them because goody-goody Josh suddenly decided to play detective? "So? What are you, a cop?" he asked sarcastically.

Josh looked over his shoulder again. "They're getting closer," he warned.

"Okay, hang on," Drake said.

Josh didn't like the warning tone of Drake's voice. "What are you going to —"

Drake slammed on the brake and clutch at the same time, turning the wheel hard to the left. Tires screeching, the Viper did a wild 180-degree turn, leaving skid marks in its wake. Drake downshifted and sped back up the street in the opposite direction.

Josh was still screaming "dooooooooooooooooo?" when they whizzed by the sedan.

Brice watched them fly by from the sedan's passenger seat. "Turn around," he ordered Deegan.

Deegan turned the wheel to the left, but the sedan couldn't make the U-turn. They hit the curb.

The Viper was a block away already.

"Hurry. C'mon," Brice yelled.

Deegan shifted into reverse. "Don't yell at me like that," he said. "And would it kill you to say please?"

Brice gritted his teeth. "Hurry. Please," he fumed.

Deegan started to back up, but a cement truck stopped behind the car, blocking them in. Deegan pounded on the horn, but it was too late.

Drake and Josh were getting away.

"Drake, Josh — I'm back," Megan called, opening the door of the Presidential Suite. There was no answer. She grabbed a bottle of water from the minifridge and looked around. A chair was turned over, and Josh's laptop and bag were on the floor, along with an empty soda can.

"Drake? Josh?" she said again. Still no answer. "Sure," Megan said to herself. "They mess up my room and then leave me here while they go out and play in Hollywood." But she wasn't going to let them get to her. "Whatever," she said. Then she spotted the room service menu.

Megan picked up the phone and hit the room service button while she looked over the menu. "I'd like to order up some dinner. I'll have some macaroni and cheese, and a shrimp cocktail, and . . ." She flipped through the menu, looking for desserts. "Do you have chocolate cake?" she asked. She listened for a minute, then smiled. "Excellent. Bring me a big piece."

Megan was about to hang up when another idea came to her. She had never had a massage, but her mom was always going on about how great they were. Every time her mom went on vacation, she made sure to stay in hotels where she could get a massage. "Can I get a massage in this hotel?" she asked. "In my room?" Wow, she didn't even have to go anywhere. "Cool."

Megan hung up with a big smile. "I love it here," she said out loud.

*   *   *

Drake and Josh cruised along in the Viper, not sure where to go. They knew they had to warn Megan to lock the door and not let anybody into the hotel room. Josh had his cell phone to his ear, but all he heard was an annoying *buzz buzz buzz*.

"You get Megan yet?" Drake asked.

"No. The phone in her room is still busy." Josh flipped the phone closed. "I can't believe we're in L.A. driving a stolen car."

Drake shook his head. "It's not stolen," he said.

"Stolen!" Josh insisted.

"We borrowed it," Drake argued. "Which is a perfectly reasonable choice when you're trying to avoid being attacked by two maniacs."

"I guess," Josh said with a worried sigh. "You think the police will understand?"

"Yeah. We just have to tell them that we were minding our own business and . . ." Drake was about to learn if his theory was correct. He heard a police siren. Drake checked the rearview mirror. "And speaking of the police . . ."

An SUV with tinted windows and a blue flashing light was right behind them.

Josh sighed. He hoped Drake was right about the police understanding. "Dude, you'd better pull over."

"Right." Drake slowed down and pulled the Viper over to the side of the road. The SUV came to a stop behind them. Two men in dark suits approached the car.

"FBI," said one of the men, holding up his ID.

The other one did the same.

"Oh," Drake said, shocked, raising his hands over his head.

Josh freaked out. The FBI was much more serious than the police. "Ohhhh," he said.

"Look, I can explain why we took this," Drake said.

"We're victims of circumstance," Josh added.

"Would you step out of the vehicle, please," said one of the agents.

Drake and Josh exchanged scared looks, then did as they were told.

"Listen, we didn't really *steal* this car," Josh said.

"There were goons chasing us," Drake explained. "We had to get away."

"We know all about it," said the first agent.

Josh was amazed — and relieved. "You do?"

"Listen, guys," said the agent. "You're not in any trouble. You did the right thing."

Drake gave Josh an "I told you so" look.

"We just need you to come with us to head-quarters so you can help us identify the men who assaulted you."

"Sure, no problem," Drake answered. He glanced at the Viper. Man, that was a fast car, and he had done some really cool driving in it. As soon as he was rich and famous, he'd buy one of his own.

"Let's do it!" Josh said. This was going to be exciting. He and Drake were going to help the FBI bring down some serious bad guys. And they weren't even in trouble for stealing a car. How cool was that?

The FBI agents led the brothers toward the SUV.

"Is there gong to be a police sketch artist there?" Josh asked. "Because I have an amazing memory for faces."

"That's great," said the agent. But he didn't seem to mean it.

"You know," Josh continued. "They were very interested in this G-O. I'm not sure why, but I have several theories. The big one —"

The agent opened the door to the SUV. The brothers found themselves face-to-face with Brice and Deegan.

"What's going on here?" Drake asked.

Josh's eyes widened in disbelief. "Why, you guys are the two —"

Brice cut him off. "Shut up," he snarled.

Josh started to back up. He looked at the FBI agents, who were smiling, and then at Drake. "I don't really think they are with the FBI," he said, in a scared, high-pitched voice.

"Ya think?" Drake answered. Man, Josh had a bad habit of stating the obvious — especially in dangerous situations.

Deegan reached forward and grabbed the G-O from Josh's hand. The brothers tried to run, but Brice held Josh by his shirt and tried to shove him into the car, while Deegan seized Drake. Josh threw himself over the roof of the car and tried to grab hold of something, but Brice was bigger and stronger. He rammed into Josh's legs, making Josh pop up and down on the roof like a jack-in-the-box. Finally, Brice managed to shove Josh all the way into the backseat. Deegan did the same with Drake.

Josh made one last escape attempt. He opened his door and tried to jump out. But by that time, Brice and Deegan had jumped into the front seat and started the car. Deegan grabbed Josh by the collar of his shirt and pulled him back into the car.

The SUV sped off, followed by the fake FBI agents in the Viper. The brothers had no idea where they were going, why exactly that G-O was so important, or even who these guys were. They only knew they were in danger — serious danger.

CHAPTER TEN

Megan flipped through channels on the giant plasma-screen TV. Something on the floor caught her eye. Which one of her brothers had dropped his wallet while he was knocking over chairs? she wondered. But the driver's license inside wasn't Drake's or Josh's. It belonged to some guy named Brice McCrary. Who was that? Curious, Megan ran her thumb across the bills inside and pulled out a slip of paper. An address — 18141 E. Addison — was scrawled on it. Was that where her brothers were?

The SUV pulled up in front of what looked like an abandoned warehouse. The Viper pulled in behind them, blocking in the SUV. A few vans were parked in the lot, along with the sedan Brice and Deegan had been driving when they chased Drake and Josh from the hotel. The sign outside the building read 18141 E. ADDISON.

Brice and Deegan dragged Drake and Josh to a door.

"We're here," Brice said into a walkie-talkie.

Drake and Josh tried to hide their panic as another guy slid open the huge steel door. Josh guessed he was the one in charge. Brice and Deegan waited for instructions.

He glared at all four of them. "Bring them in," he ordered.

Brice pushed Drake and Josh into a grungy warehouse. The walls were covered with graffiti. There was a huge high-tech-looking machine sitting in the middle of the floor, like a cross between a giant copy machine and an airport X-ray scanner. Workers hurried around, using forklifts to move wooden pallets of blank paper around the room. A computer buzzed and clicked.

"Where is it?" snapped the guy in charge.

"Here it is, Milo." Deegan reached into his pocket and handed him the G-O.

Milo punched the controls, then turned to Deegan with a smile. "I think we have our key."

Josh decided it was time to negotiate with this Milo person. "Look, sir." He put his hands on his hips and tried to sound tough, but inside he was quivering. "I don't know what this is about."

"Be quiet, Josh," Drake urged.

Josh ignored him. "But I am in the Honor Society."

Drake stared at his brother in disbelief. These guys were definitely not the type to care about things like the Honor Society. "Stop talking," Drake said. Josh was only digging them in deeper.

But Josh didn't stop. "And my father happens to be the weatherman for KXTV in San Diego."

"Dad's a goof, Josh," Drake said. The panic was growing in his voice.

"So, I demand that you return us to —"

But Josh wasn't in a position to demand anything. Milo cut him off, pointing to a door on the other side of the warehouse. "Lock them in there," he ordered.

Brice and Deegan shoved them into the room. The brothers crumpled onto the concrete floor just before Deegan slammed and locked the door.

They were trapped.

Josh looked around at the small, dirty room. He

was surrounded by wooden crates, but nothing that gave him a clue as to what was happening on the other side of the locked door. He paced while Drake sat slumped in the corner.

Hours passed. Drake started pacing while Josh sat, staring at the wall. Eventually they both fell asleep, but woke up when they tried to turn over on the concrete floor. Josh's arm was draped over his brother.

"What time is it?" Drake jumped to his feet.

"Two in the morning," Josh said, shaking off the sleep.

"Man, I'm supposed to play live on TRL in fifteen hours," Drake said.

Josh shook his head. What had he gotten them into with that stupid G-O? "Man, I wish I knew what they were up to," he said.

Drake noticed that one of the walls didn't quite reach the ceiling. He tapped Josh on the shoulder and pointed, in case anyone was listening. They piled wooden crates into a stack and climbed up to peer over the top of the wall.

"What is it?" Josh whispered.

"I don't know. Shhh," Drake answered.

They watched Milo pick up the G-O.

"Okay. Let's see if the information on this thing is worth what we paid." Milo connected the G-O to a computer panel on the big machine and typed in a command. Nothing happened.

Deegan leaned over his shoulder.

"Is it working or not?" Milo asked.

"I think so." Deegan hit some more keys. Codes scrolled across the computer screen. He grinned. "I think we're good to go."

Milo pressed a big green button. More lights flashed, followed by some beeps and the sound of the machine warming up. A hundred dollar bill flashed across the computer screen.

A huge sheet of hundred dollar bills shot out of the machine. "And there it is!" Milo said.

Everyone in the warehouse cheered and clapped — everyone but Drake and Josh. Sheets of bills were being printed so fast that the brothers couldn't even count them. Then the sheets were fed into another machine that cut them up into perfect stacks of hundred dollar bills.

"Whoa, look at that," Josh whispered.

Drake's jaw dropped. "It's a money machine."

Suddenly, Josh remembered the report he had heard in the airport. "Yeah, I saw a story on the news. Someone stole a U.S. currency machine from Washington three days ago."

"So what's the G-O for?" Drake asked. If these guys had a money machine, why did they need a digital music player? he wondered.

"It probably has codes on it that make the money machine work. Kind of like an electronic key."

Josh forgot to keep his voice down. Deegan noticed him peering over the wall. "Hey," he shouted. Everyone looked up.

Drake and Josh dropped to the floor. By the time Brice and Deegan opened the door to the locked room, Drake and Josh were sitting cross-legged on the floor and playing a hand-clapping game that Megan played with her girlfriends.

Josh pretended to be surprised. "Oh, hey, fellas," he said, with a big smile, not missing a beat as he clapped his hands on his knees, and then together, before slapping them one at a time against Drake's hands.

"Want to play?" Drake asked innocently, keeping the game going.

Brice and Deegan glared at them, then slammed the door.

The brothers heard the lock click. Trapped again.

Megan woke up in her big red bed the next morning to the sound of the phone ringing. "Hello," she mumbled.

"Good morning, Miss Parker. This is your wake-up call."

"Thanks," she said. Megan looked around the room. The sun was shining, and it was still the coolest hotel room she had ever seen, but it was empty. "Drake? Josh?" she called, but she could tell no one was there. Next she tried her cell phone. Maybe they had left a message while she was sleeping.

"No new messages," said the computer voice.

Megan chewed her bottom lip. She was starting to get worried. Drake and Josh wouldn't fly all the way to L.A. to make sure she was all right, and then just disappear — especially when Drake was getting ready to appear on TRL.

Something was wrong — very wrong. Megan remembered how the room had been messed up when she got back from the pool the day before. Then she pulled the piece of paper out of the wallet again. She stared at the address, wondering again if that's where her brothers were.

What if they were in trouble? They were often annoying, and they *had* put her on the wrong plane, but they were still her brothers. If they were in trouble, she had to help them.

Megan picked up Ah'lee's business card and dialed the phone.

Josh could hear the money machine spewing out bills while Drake worked on the lock with a rusty old screwdriver they had found in a corner. "Can you get it?" he asked.

"I think so," Drake whispered. "Wait." The lock clicked and Drake carefully tried the knob. It turned. "Got it!" he said.

"Yes." Josh pumped his fist in the air.

"Shhh!" Drake said. "I'm going to take a look outside." He opened the door a crack and peeked. Brice and another big guy stood guard by the main door. Everybody else was busy with the money.

"Well?" Josh asked. What was taking so long?

"There are just two of them by the door. So here's the plan." He picked up a two-by-four next to the door. "We sneak up on them, and when I yell 'now!' you hit the one on the left with this." He handed Josh the piece of wood. "And I'll hit the other one with this." Drake held up a broken lamp.

"Got it." Josh got a firm grip on the two-by-four. He had never hit anyone before, but these were bad guys and he was ready.

"When they go down," Drake said, "we run as fast as we can out the door and try to get someone's attention."

Josh nodded. "Right." He tried to sound strong and brave, and for a moment he was. He'd do this.

"You set?" Drake asked.

Josh nodded again. They crept out of the room, weapons in hand.

CHAPTER ELEVEN

Drake and Josh snuck up behind Brice and one of the fake FBI guys. Josh held the two-by-four over his head, ready to strike, and it rattled up against the chain-link fence between the two parts of the warehouse. They came to a sudden stop, their hearts pounding. The guards didn't hear them over the noise of the money machine. If the computer panel was right, these guys had already printed more than four hundred million dollars.

The brothers tiptoed the last few steps.

Drake nodded to Josh.

Josh nodded back.

"Now!" Drake yelled. He swung the lamp with all his might and hit the one guard in the head.

Josh did the same with his two-by-four, hitting Brice on the shoulder.

The guards flinched, then slowly turned and loomed over the brothers.

Drake couldn't believe it. If someone hit *him* that

hard, he'd be unconscious for days. These guys barely moved. If they weren't in such serious trouble, Drake would even be a little embarrassed. "We thought you'd fall down," he said with a wry smile.

Josh nodded and tried to smile, too. Maybe if they pretended it was all fun and games, Brice and the other guard would think they were just fooling around.

But they didn't. The next thing the boys knew, Brice had tied their hands behind their backs and thrown them to the floor in the middle of the room.

"Now I can keep an eye on you," he said. "Don't move."

Workers moved around, stepping over Drake and Josh but barely looking at them as they stacked piles of hundred dollar bills and got ready to move them out of the warehouse. The money machine was still printing. The boys exchanged worried looks. It wasn't just about missing TRL anymore. Unless someone came to their rescue — and soon — they might not get out of this mess alive.

*　　*　　*

Ah'lee's white limo drove slowly down the street. Megan peered out of the window, checking addresses.

"Wait," she said, reading the numbers off an old, brick building. "18141. This is it." She waited while Ah'lee pulled into the parking lot, then got out of the car. "Be back in a second," she said.

Megan walked up to the grungy warehouse, ready to knock on the door. Then she changed her mind. If Drake and Josh were in some kind of trouble, she'd better figure out what was going on before she charged in. She found a window covered by a metal shutter, and looked inside.

Megan's eyes bulged. Money was piled everywhere — tons and tons of money. Lots of people moved around — printing money, stacking money, counting money. But why would her brothers be here? Megan wondered.

Then she spotted them, tied up and slumped on the floor. They looked scared. She was right. They were in trouble — *serious* trouble. Megan moved away from the window before anyone could see her and flipped open her cell phone.

A 911 operator answered. "Los Angeles Police Department. What is your emergency?"

"My name is Megan Parker and I'm at 18141 East Addison. I need cops — now."

"Please repeat your message. Your cell phone is breaking up," the operator said.

"I'm at 18141 East Addison," Megan shouted. "They've got my brothers tied up inside, and they're printing tons of money." All she heard was static. "Hey, did you hear that? Hello?"

There was no answer. The call went dead. Megan tried to redial, but all her cell phone said was NO SIGNAL.

Josh was desperate to get his brother out of that warehouse — alive. He looked around for anything that might help. Suddenly, he spotted something. He caught Drake's eye. "Look behind you," he whispered, nodding toward something against the wall.

Drake looked over his shoulder. Half of a pair of old, broken scissors was lodged under a rusty paint can. Drake stretched his leg out as far as it would go and tried to slide the half-scissor toward them, but his shoe didn't reach. They'd have to squirm across the floor.

Josh whistled and coughed to cover the sound of Drake's movement. The people around them were so caught up in their jobs that they didn't notice the brothers slide across the floor — just far enough for Drake to reach the scissor with his foot. They made sure no one was behind them. Josh kept whistling while Drake slid the scissor into his hand and started sawing on the rope around his wrists. Then he slipped the scissor to Josh.

"Okay, here," Drake said. "Don't cut all the way through. Make it look like you're still tied up."

Josh sliced at his ropes, leaving a few strings attached so he couldn't forget and move his arms until it was time to break free.

The numbers on the money machine were close to five hundred million dollars.

"Half a billion dollars," Brice said with a huge smile.

"I think life in Brazil is going to be pretty sweet," Milo answered.

Deegan nodded in the direction of their prisoners. "What about them?"

Milo headed toward Drake and Josh, followed by Brice and Deegan. Josh dropped the scissor. Did they know he and Drake were almost loose?

"What's up, guys?" Milo asked.

"Are you going to let us go now?" Drake asked, hopefully.

"We swear we won't say a word about your money or anything!" Josh added, trying to sound convincing. Why had he bragged to those FBI guys about having such a good memory for faces?

Milo stared at them with a grim expression. There was no way he could trust these two. "I wish I could believe that," Milo said.

Drake swallowed. Cold fear crept down his spine. He did not like the look on Milo's face.

Josh's eyes darted nervously from Milo to Brice and back again.

"Well." Milo thought for a minute, then broke into a happy grin. "I hope you boys are very good swimmers."

Good swimmers? The brothers exchanged scared looks. What was Milo going to do, dump them in the ocean? They had to find a way out of here.

Milo turned his back on them. "All right," he said, in a loud voice. "Get the money loaded on to the vans. We're moving out."

Megan checked her watch and lifted the metal shutter again. She saw Milo standing over her brothers. They looked even more scared than before. She tried her phone again. There was still no signal, and still no police.

She couldn't wait anymore. She opened the door a crack and snuck in. Workers were moving the money out of the warehouse and into vans. She spotted a trash bin and ducked behind it.

Drake and Josh were looking around for an escape route when Drake spotted Megan. His eyes widened in fear. Oh, no, now they had somehow gotten their little sister involved with the bad guys. He nudged Josh, then whispered to her, "What are you doing?"

"Shhh!" Megan held her finger over her lips. She scanned the room for something — *anything* — that might help her brothers. Then she spotted two humungous fans on the opposite side of the warehouse. She might be able to use them to distract the bad guys long enough to help Drake and Josh escape. But first she had to find a way to turn them on.

Drake and Josh watched in horror as Megan ducked from money stack to money stack, hiding behind each one as she made her way to the opposite wall. There were some big industrial switches just under the fans. One had a label above it that read FANS. It looked old and rusty, but Megan had to hope it would work.

Megan looked from the fans to the money and then over to Drake and Josh. She took a big breath and used all her strength to flip the switch.

The fans whirred into action. Suddenly, there was a giant blizzard of money flying all around the warehouse.

"Hey, what's going on?" workers yelled. They ran around, trying to catch the money, but it was flying too fast. All of their neat stacks were in the air or on the floor.

"Who turned on the fans?" Brice yelled.

"I don't know," Deegan said, glaring at Drake and Josh. But they were too far away to have caused this nightmare.

"Where's the switch?" someone yelled.

"Find it and turn them off," Milo ordered.

Megan grabbed a fire extinguisher off the wall and banged it against the switch until the switch wouldn't move anymore. There was no way those guys were going to be able to turn the fans off. Then she tucked the extinguisher under her arm and ducked behind a wooden crate.

Brice ran to the switch. He tried to turn the fans off, but the switch was stuck. He pulled and pushed and struggled, but it wouldn't budge. The fans continued to spin at full speed. Tens of thousands of dollars swirled through the air.

Drake got Josh's attention. Everyone was so busy trying to keep the money from flying away that no one was watching them. It was time to get Megan and get out of here. "Let's go!" he said.

They jumped up, shook the ropes off their wrists, and ran toward Megan and the exit. But one of the thugs noticed them.

"Get the kids!" he yelled. "Get the kids!"

Drake and Josh ran one way, only to run into Brice and Deegan head-on. They ran the other way, but wherever they turned, big men blocked their path.

"C'mon, c'mon, dude. Let's go." Josh picked up a heavy bag and threw it hard into someone's stomach.

The fight waged on. Drake and Josh managed to stay out of Brice and Deegan's grasp, but they couldn't find Megan and they couldn't make it to the exit. Every time they turned around, someone blocked their way.

Megan had forgotten all about the danger. She was in a corner, catching flying hundred dollar bills and stuffing them into her backpack. "I love L.A.!" she said.

Drake jumped up onto a platform and started throwing metal barrels at anyone who tried to follow.

One of the thugs had Josh in a headlock. "Help, Drake!" he yelled.

Drake grabbed hold of a rope and hurled himself through the air, hitting the thug in the chest with his feet. The guy fell flat on his back, banging his head on the concrete.

One down.

But there were a lot more bad guys, and the ones who weren't trying to grab the money were after Drake and Josh. At least they didn't know Megan was there.

Drake saw someone coming up behind his brother,

ready to bash him over the head. "Josh, run!" Drake yelled.

Josh slipped away and climbed up onto a scaffold. Deegan was right behind him.

"Josh, look out!" Drake yelled.

Josh grabbed a pipe and swung it, knocking Deegan to the floor. "Yeah!" Josh pumped his fist in the air. But now Drake was the one in trouble. One of the fake FBI guys had him in a headlock.

"Hang on, Drake. I'm coming." Josh let out a Tarzan yell and tried to swing to Drake's rescue, but the rope broke. Josh crumpled to the floor in a heap. He looked for Drake, but he had disappeared under a pile of thugs who swarmed over him, like football players in a giant tackle. With another Tarzan yell, Josh hurled himself on top of them, knocking the whole group to the floor.

Drake and Josh did their best to stay out of the men's grasp, find Megan, and get out of there, but they were badly outnumbered. Escape seemed impossible. The best they could do was fight them off — for now.

Brice got knocked over the head and fell on top of

the money pile Megan was hiding behind. She stopped catching bills for a second and pounded Brice on the head with her fire extinguisher. He slipped to the floor. Megan went back to catching hundreds while her brothers kept up the fight.

But Brice's blow to the head landed him right in front of a sledgehammer. He dragged it over to the fans and used it to knock the switch loose. The swirling air slowed, then stopped. Milo's goons cornered Drake and Josh. They stood back-to-back in the middle of the room.

Josh turned and slugged the person behind him, only to discover it was his brother. "Oh, Drake. I'm sorry."

But they had bigger problems.

They were surrounded, they were exhausted, and there was no way out.

CHAPTER TWELVE

Suddenly, the doors flew open with a bang and the police rushed in. "Nobody move! Hands behind your heads."

Milo and his gang gaped at each other in horror. Now they were the ones with no place to run. One by one, they let go of Drake and Josh and put their hands over their heads.

The brothers eyed each other with relief as two detectives led them outside.

The two detectives, Baxter and Jamison, stood with Drake, Josh, and Megan as Milo's gang was handcuffed and forced into the police cars. Lights flashed and sirens blared as the cops drove off with the criminals. Milo glared at the brothers as he was led to a car.

"That's the leader — Milo McCrary," Detective Baxter explained. "He's one of the FBI's ten most wanted."

"That comes as no surprise. He is not friendly." Josh crossed his arms over his chest in disgust. He couldn't believe that guy was going to dump him and Drake into the ocean.

"No, he's not," Baxter agreed. "You're lucky we got here when we did. "

Drake and Josh both shuddered with relief. They knew how close they had come to being seriously hurt.

"That was pretty smart of you guys, turning those fans on," Detective Jamison added.

Megan rolled her eyes and snorted. "Yeah," she said sarcastically. "They're geniuses."

Another police car pulled up. A man got out of the backseat, talking on a cell phone. The detective with him pointed at the red Viper, then to Drake and Josh.

"Who's that guy?" Josh asked.

"I think that's Tony Hawk's manager," Mr. Jamison answered.

"Tony Hawk? The skateboarder?" Drake said.

"What's his manager doing here?" Josh asked.

"Well, I imagine he came to get Tony's car back," Mr. Jamison said, raising his eyebrows.

Drake and Josh stared at the Viper, then at each other.

"We stole Tony Hawk's Viper," Josh said.

The manager walked over. "Are you the guys who took Tony's car?" he asked.

Drake and Josh talked over each other, trying to explain. After all they had been through, were they going to get in trouble for stealing the car?

"Okay, we're soooooo sorry," Drake said. "The only reason we took his car was because these crazy goons were chasing us."

"Please don't have us arrested," Josh sputtered. "We're very nice people. We wouldn't have taken his car if those guys —"

The manager interrupted. "Whoa, easy. The detective called my office and explained everything. It's cool."

It's cool? "Tony's not mad?" Drake asked.

The manager laughed. "No. He said if two goons were chasing him, he'd steal a car, too."

Drake was totally relieved. "Hey, who wouldn't?"

"It's a natural response," Josh added.

Megan shook her head. She couldn't stand around and listen to her brothers make idiots out of themselves in front of Tony Hawk's manager. She had a plane to catch, and she wasn't going to let them make her miss her flight — *again*.

"Okay, if you guys don't need me anymore, I'm going to Denver. Gentlemen," she said, as she nodded good-bye to the detectives. Then she turned to her brothers. "Dweebs."

"Hey, wait," Drake said. "Don't you need help in getting to Denver?"

"Yeah," Megan snorted. Hadn't she just saved her brothers from a band of counterfeiters? Counterfeiters who were on the FBI's most wanted list? "I need *your* help." She climbed into Ah'lee's white limo and left for the airport.

Watching Megan drive off in a limousine jogged something in Josh's brain. He and Drake were supposed to be somewhere, too. "Aw, man!" Josh said, slapping himself on the forehead.

"What?" Drake asked.

"TRL! You're supposed to go on in —" Josh checked his watch "— twenty-five minutes."

"Oh, that's right," Drake said, remembering.

"Where?" Detective Baxter asked.

Josh snapped his fingers. "Umm, umm."

Drake grabbed Josh's shoulders and gave them a shake, as if that would make him remember. "Where is it?"

"Umm," Josh thought some more, then snapped his fingers again. "Sunset Studios!"

Detective Jamison shook his head. "That's a forty-five-minute drive from here."

"We're not going to make it," Drake said. He couldn't believe that he was going to be a no-show on TRL. He was ruining his music career before he even got started.

Tony Hawk's manager spoke up. "Well, you might make it. With a fast car."

Drake and Josh exchanged excited looks. Did that mean what they thought it meant?

"You'll let us drive Tony's car?" Drake asked.

"Why not? He's got three of them."

Maybe I do have a shot at making it to TRL after all, Drake thought. "Awesome!"

"Thanks," Josh added.

Drake and Josh needed more than a fast car to get

there on time. The manager turned to the detectives. "Hey, why don't you give these guys a police escort?" he asked.

"I don't really think I could," Detective Baxter said.

But the manager wasn't giving up. "C'mon. They helped you capture a guy on the FBI's most wanted list. Go on, give them an escort."

Drake held his breath. Josh crossed his fingers.

"Will you get me an autograph from Tony?" Baxter asked. The manager nodded. Baxter smiled then called two motorcycle cops over. "Get these guys to Sunset Studios in Hollywood — as fast as you can."

"This is insane!" Drake yelled, running for Tony's car. "I'm going to be on TRL!"

"Yeah, if we get there in time. Let's go," Josh said.

The brothers vaulted over the doors and landed perfectly in the front seat.

Drake turned the key, and the engine roared to life. Josh turned on the stereo. They buckled their seat belts. Then they each grabbed a pair of Tony's sunglasses from the console and slipped them on.

They were ready.

"Hit it, brother," Josh said with a grin.

The motorcycles pulled out, sirens wailing. Drake peeled out right behind them. They had twenty-three minutes to make a forty-five-minute drive. Even with a police escort and Tony Hawk's superfast car, would they make it?

CHAPTER THIRTEEN

At Sunset Studios, the production crew got the set ready while Drake's band warmed up on stage.

"Okay, let's hurry up, people," the stage manager said. "We go live in twenty-three minutes."

Mitch walked into the studio. "Is that Drake Parker's band?" he asked.

"Yeah," the stage manager told him.

Mitch looked them over. He remembered them from Josh's DVD, but someone was missing. "Where's Drake?" he asked.

The stage manager shrugged.

He'd better get here, Mitch thought. He needed a live act — and soon. He paced, waiting.

"Okay," the stage manager said, checking his watch. "Eighteen minutes."

Drake and Josh raced through the streets of L.A., led by the motorcycle cops. They flew past famous Hollywood landmarks. The cars they passed were just a blur, Drake was driving so fast. He pushed the gas pedal to the floor and sped through an intersection, avoiding a crash by a split second.

"Whoa," Josh yelled, clutching the dashboard.

Drake checked his watch. Just five minutes to go.

Then four.

Then three.

This can't be happening, he thought. He couldn't be this close to his big break and then lose it. He downshifted and pressed the gas pedal a little harder. The speedometer shot up over a hundred.

Inside the studio, the crew waited. The band paced nervously. Mitch fumed. He couldn't believe he had taken a chance on a totally unknown kid. Drake Parker could forget TRL and MTV forever if he wasn't here in time. Mitch would make sure he spent the rest of his career playing in nothing better than bathrooms.

"Live in three minutes," the stage manager said.

The motorcycle cops peeled off with a wave when they saw the Sunset Studios sign. Drake pulled into the lot, but a gate blocked his way.

A production assistant ran up to the guard. "Let him through!" he yelled, then grabbed his walkie-talkie. "He's here! Get his guitar."

The guard lifted the gate and the Viper screeched into the parking lot, coming to a stop in front of the entrance.

"Live in two minutes," the stage manager said.

Mitch had had it. This kid had totally flaked out on him. Not only had he ruined his own career, but Drake Parker and his manager brother were making Mitch look bad. "Okay, that's it," he said, pulling out his cell phone. "I'm calling New York and telling them to pull the plug on this."

A production assistant ducked in. "He's here."

"He's lucky," Mitch muttered. Drake Parker had some serious things to learn about being a professional, he thought. If he weren't totally stuck for a live act, he'd send these guys right back to where they came from.

Drake leaped out of the car and ran into the studio, followed by Josh and two production assistants.

"Hi. Sorry I'm late," Drake said, slipping his guitar over his head.

"We'll discuss that later," Mitch answered.

"Thirty seconds," the stage manager said.

Mitch pointed. "Get in front of those cameras."

Drake jumped onstage. Someone plugged his guitar into the amp while Josh adjusted the mike, then fixed Drake's hair.

"I look okay?" Drake asked.

"Awesome," Josh said.

"Ten seconds!" the stage manager yelled.

Josh was standing right in front of the camera.

"Josh. Off!" Mitch yelled.

But Josh needed a minute with his brother. "Are you going to make me proud?" Josh asked with a smile.

Drake grinned. He trusted his talent and his band. All they needed was a break, and Josh had gotten one for them. "Watch this," Drake said confidently.

"All right!" Josh pumped his fist in the air and stood behind the cameras with Mitch.

This was it.

Josh kept his eyes on the television monitor. TRL's host in New York grabbed the mike.

"Okay, right here for the first time on TRL," he said. "He's an up-and-coming artist from San Diego. You may not have heard of him, but you will. Let's make some noise for Drake Parker!"

Kids in both studios — mostly beautiful girls, Drake noticed — screamed and cheered. The stage manager pointed to Drake, and he and his band launched into a song.

> *Hollywood girl*
> *Is lost again*
> *All of her hopes left her stranded*

Josh and Mitch watched a split-screen TV monitor that had four pictures from four different cameras. Drake looked great. And the studio audience in New York was clearly loving Drake as much as the one in L.A.

The studio audience was going wild. Josh couldn't help it; he was so happy and excited that he launched into his own crazy dance — arms and legs flying. Mitch turned with an amused expression and Josh stopped short, but Mitch was grinning, too. This was going great!

Then picked it up again for the chorus:

Cause in this town
Can't find up but I found down
In the city life
Can't turn around
I can't give up I feel too proud
Under the city lights

Drake played the last chord and they were off. The crowd went wild — screaming, dancing, cheering, and clapping. Josh leaned over and gave the stage manager a big fat kiss on the forehead. Drake took his guitar off and ran over to Josh.

"Well?" he asked. Drake knew it was good. But he wanted to hear it from his manager.

Josh had a huge grin on his face. "Dude, awesome! Best ever."

"Thanks, dude."

Mitch walked over and shook Drake's hand. "Mitch Gordon," he said. "I book talent for MTV."

"Right. Thanks so much for having me on," Drake said.

"Thank you. You're good. You should have a record deal."

"I'm available," Drake said.

"Oh, is he available," Josh added, practically bouncing with excitement.

"*So* available," Drake added — just to be sure Mitch got the point.

"Well, if you can arrange a trip to New York, I can hook you up with Alan Krim."

Drake couldn't believe it. This was amazing. "At Spin City Records?"

"I think he'll be impressed with you." Mitch turned to Josh. "Hey, thanks for being so pushy in the men's room. You saved my butt."

Josh grinned. "Any time."

The stage manager interrupted. "Mitch. Your lunch is here."

"Gotta run," Mitch said. "See you guys in New York."

Josh watched him jog off, then turned to his brother. "Dude, I cannot believe what's happened to us in the last couple of days."

"Yeah," Drake nodded. "I don't think you'll have too much trouble writing about your greatest adventure ever."

"Yeah." Josh had forgotten all about his creative writing class and his fears that his life was too boring to write about. "Oh, yeah," he said again. He certainly had enough adventures now to fill three stories — putting Megan on the wrong flight, catching the counterfeiters, and getting his brother a shot on MTV. "Hey, so how does it feel to play for millions of people on national television?" Josh asked.

Drake answered with a question. "How does it feel to be the best band manager ever?"

The brothers looked around to see if anyone was watching, then shared a quick brotherly hug.

"Well, brothah," Josh said. "It's just you and me in Hollywood. What do you want to do?"

Just then, two pretty girls rushed up — one blonde and one brunette.

"Drake! You were so awesome," the brunette said.

"Thanks," Drake said. He usually kept the pretty girls to himself, but Josh deserved some major thanks. "Hey, this is my brother, Josh."

"Can we hang out with you guys?" the brunette asked.

"Please?" pleaded the blonde.

Drake and Josh smiled at each other over the girls' heads. Two beautiful girls wanted to hang out with them. Who were they to say no?

"Yes, you can," they said at the same time.

They had rescued Megan and brought down a major crime ring — well, with Megan's help. Drake had gotten his first big break and maybe a record deal. And now they were about to set off for an evening in Hollywood with two beautiful girls.

Life was good.

The four of them jumped into Tony Hawk's Viper and drove off into the sunset.